The Clover County Carrot Contest

BY JOHN HIMMELMAN

Silver Press

For Deborah Michel and Marcia Leonard, who played
no small part in bringing the Fix-it Family to life.
—J.H.

Library of Congress Cataloging-in-Publication Data

Himmelman, John.
The Clover County carrot contest / by John Himmelman.
p. cm.—(The Fix-it family)
Summary: The members of the Wright family compete in growing
carrots for the big Clover County contest.
[1. Carrots—Fiction. 2. Gardening—Fiction. 3. Contests—
Fiction. 4. Beavers—Fiction.] I. Title. II. Series: Himmelman,
John, Fix-it family.
PZ7.H5686Cl 1991
[E]—dc20   90-47200
ISBN 0-671-69637-8 LSB   CIP
ISBN 0-671-69641-6   AC

Produced by Small Packages, Inc.
Copyright © 1991 by John Himmelman and Small Packages, Inc.
All rights reserved. No part of this book may be used
or reproduced in any manner whatsoever without written
permission from the publisher.
Published by Silver Press, a division of
Silver Burdett Press, Inc.
Simon & Schuster, Inc.
Prentice Hall Bldg., Englewood Cliffs, NJ 07632.
Printed in the United States of America.
10 9 8 7 6 5 4 3 2 1

The Fix-It Family

Orville and Willa Wright

own a fix-it shop.

If something is broken,

they will repair it.

They can fix anything!

They are also inventors.

And their children—

Alexander, Graham, and Belle—

like inventing things, too.

CHAPTER ONE
The Carrot Contest

It was that time of year again.

Every summer, Clover County

held a carrot-growing contest.

Every summer, Orville and Willa

were busy fixing

everyone else's gardening tools.

"Maybe this year *we* should

enter the contest," said Willa.

"That sounds like fun,"

said Orville.

Willa went to the store.

There were only five packets
of carrot seeds left.

She bought them all.

"Alexander, Graham, and Belle
might want to enter, too,"
she thought.

She was right.

"There will be four prizes

in the contest," explained Willa.

"One for the biggest carrot.

One for the most orangy carrot.

One for the tastiest carrot.

And one for the crunchiest carrot."

"Will there be a prize

for the best dancing carrot?"

joked Graham.

"Oh, don't be silly,"

said Alexander.

"Silly, silly," said Belle.

The Wrights went to work.

Orville wanted to grow

the biggest carrot.

He invented a machine

to keep away bugs and weeds.

Willa tested all the soil

in the backyard.

She wanted to find

just the right spot

to grow the most orangy carrot.

Alexander wanted the prize

for the tastiest carrot.

He made a special drink

to feed his carrots.

Graham made crunchy noises
into a tape recorder.

He put special underground speakers
next to his carrot patch.

He was going to teach his carrots
to be the crunchiest.

Finally, they were all ready
to plant their carrot seeds.
Belle came out of the house.
She carried a wooden spoon
and her packet of seeds.

"Where is your invention?"

asked Graham.

"Right here," said Belle.

"It is a carrot-hole digger."

She scooped out

a few spoonfuls of dirt.

She dropped the seeds

into the holes.

She patted the dirt back down

with the spoon.

"All done," she said.

And she went back into the house.

CHAPTER TWO
Secret Helpers

Several weeks passed by.

Orville's carrots

were growing very large.

Willa's carrots

were growing a nice shade of orange.

Alexander's carrots

were growing tastier and tastier.

"Don't taste them too often,"

warned Willa,

"or you will get a prize

for the tiniest carrots."

Graham held up one of his carrots.

"Listen to this," he said.

He took a big bite.

CRUNCH! went the carrot.

Alexander covered his ears.

"That is the noisiest carrot

I've ever heard," he said.

"Thank you," said Graham.

Belle sat by her carrot patch.

Two tiny leaves

stuck out of the ground.

Only one little carrot

was coming up.

"My carrots just need

a little more time,"

she said.

But her family felt bad for her.
"Her carrots will never grow
in this spot," thought Willa.

She waited for everyone to go inside.
Then she mixed some of her good soil
into Belle's soil.

Later that afternoon,

Graham came out to the garden.

"Big brother to the rescue,"

he said.

He dug up his speakers.

He hid them next to Belle's carrot

and tiptoed away.

Then Alexander came out
to feed his carrots.
"Poor Belle," he thought.
"Her carrots could use some help."
So every day, he secretly poured
some of his special drink
on Belle's carrot patch.

And every night,

Orville secretly moved his machine

next to Belle's little carrot.

"If it worked for my carrots,

it will work for her carrots,"

he thought.

A few more weeks passed by.

Belle's one carrot stayed the same.

And no new carrots popped up.

But Belle was not worried.

"It just needs a little more time,"

she said.

CHAPTER THREE
Big, Orangy, Tasty, Crunchy

At last it was time

for the Clover County Carrot Contest.

The Wrights picked their best carrots

to enter into the contest.

Not Belle.

She sat beside her one tiny carrot.

"I don't understand it,"
said Alexander.

"Me, neither," said Graham.

"I wonder what went wrong,"
said Orville.

"Yes, me, too," said Willa.

"Do not worry," said Belle.

"It is almost ready.

It will finish growing on the way

to the contest."

"Not if we pull it out of the dirt,"

said Orville.

"Then we can bring the dirt, too!"

said Belle.

Orville and Willa

dug around Belle's carrot.

They put the big lump of dirt

in a wheelbarrow.

"It will have to do some fast growing,"
Alexander whispered to Orville.

"I know," Orville whispered back.

He pushed the wheelbarrow

to the contest.

"Just in time," said the judge.

He looked at Orville's carrot.

"My, this certainly is the largest

carrot I've seen today,"

he said.

Then he looked at Willa's carrot.

"And this is surely

the most delightful shade of orange."

Alexander's carrot was next.

The judge tasted it.

Then he took another taste.

And another.

"Mmmmm, most delicious," he said.

Then Graham handed the judge

a pair of earmuffs.

"You'd better wear these

when you taste my carrot,"

he said.

The judge took a bite

out of Graham's carrot.

CRRRRUNCH! went the carrot.

"That was a loud one!"

laughed the judge.

"Well, I've made my decision...."

"Wait!" said Belle.

"You have not seen my carrot."

The judge looked at the wheelbarrow.

"There is a carrot in there?"

He pulled the tiny leaves.

The carrot did not budge.

Then he gave it a big yank.

"WOW!" said the crowd.

The judge was holding

the biggest, most orangy carrot

in all of Clover County!

He took a taste.

"This is also the tastiest
and crunchiest carrot
I've ever eaten,"
he said between crunches.
"Your carrot wins
all four blue ribbons!"

"See," said Belle.

"It just needed a little more time."

"And a little bit of help,"

thought each of the Wrights.

It was a proud day

for all of them.

The End